Princess Cressida and the Mermaids' Gift

by
Deborah Grace White

Once upon a time...

...there was a princess named **Cressida**.
She was a princess of the land, and she
lived in a beautiful castle by the ocean.

Princess Cressida loved the ocean. Every day she would go down to the water to play in the shallows with her best friend, **Princess Crystal**.

There was something very special about **Princess Crystal**. She was a princess of the sea. She was a MERMAID.

And she loved to swim up to the shallows to play in the water with **Princess Cressida**.

1

One day, **Princess Cressida** was building sandcastles on the beach when **Princess Crystal** appeared in the water.

"Princess Cressida!" she called. "My undersea kingdom is in trouble. Will you help us?"

"Of course I want to help," said **Princess Cressida**, splashing into the shallows. "But how can I, when I can't dive below the water like you can?"

"I can help you dive below the water!" said **Princess Crystal**.

Then she told **Princess Cressida** about the mermaids' greatest gift.

"Every mermaid has the power to give *one person* a very special gift," said the sea princess. "It's part of our magic."

"A magic gift?" **Princess Cressida** asked.

"Yes!" said **Princess Crystal**. "The magic gift makes the person have legs on land, but a tail in the water."

"You mean," **Princess Cressida** asked slowly, "it makes them a mermaid?"

"That's right," said **Princess Crystal**. "**Princess Cressida**," she added solemnly, "you are my very best friend, and I want to give you the magic gift. Would you like it?"

Princess Cressida's eyes were wide, but she didn't hesitate. "Yes," she said, nodding eagerly.

Then, before she could blink, a strange tingling started in her legs.

Looking down, she saw pink scales growing on her skin, then all of a sudden—**POP!** Her legs turned into a shiny pink mermaid tail!

Princess Cressida could hardly believe it! She launched herself into the water, twisting and splashing and admiring her new tail.

She could move so quickly through the water, and it felt warm instead of cold.

It was the most incredible thing that had ever happened to her!

"Come on!" said **Princess Crystal**, and the two girls—now two mermaids—dove into the murky dark depths.

Only, it wasn't murky or dark. **Princess Cressida** had eyes like a mermaid now, and she could see perfectly through the water, even as they went deeper and deeper. And she didn't have to hold her breath either. She could breathe underwater!

Soon she saw a pearly glow at the bottom of the ocean, and she got her first ever look at **Princess Crystal**'s beautiful underwater kingdom.

"You have a castle, just like ours!" **Princess Cressida** said, amazed that she could speak underwater.

"We do," **Princess Crystal** agreed. "But we're all in trouble."

"What happened?" Princess Cressida asked.

"Some sharks got into our city," the mermaid princess explained. "My father scared them away, but somehow he dropped his trident while he was chasing them. And now it's gone! We can't find it anywhere, and we think someone might have stolen it."

"Oh no," said Princess Cressida. "That sounds bad."

"It is bad," said **Princess Crystal**. "The trident is magical, and without it, my father can't control the waves and currents. Since it went missing, the water has been doing strange things. That's why we think someone stole it!"

"We have to find it," said Princess Cressida, determined. Without another word, they flipped their tails, pushing themselves through the water to join the merpeople who were searching everywhere for the trident.

Princess Cressida was swimming over a clump of seaweed when she caught sight of a little merboy, huddled up on the ocean floor below her. He wasn't searching for the trident like everyone else. He had a sad frown, and he looked like he'd been crying. She dove down to him.

"Are you all right?" she asked.

He looked up at her, and he looked scared. She looked at his big, worried eyes, and she suddenly remembered a time she had felt worried, too. It was when she had taken her mother's crown without asking.

She hadn't meant any harm. But her mother had been so upset when she discovered it was missing, **Princess Cressida** had been scared to admit she had it.

She looked at the boy closely. Maybe he was worried because he had done something wrong, too.

"Do you know something about the missing trident?" she asked. He looked more scared than ever. "It's all right," she said kindly. "I want to help you." He still didn't say anything, so she tried again. "I can see you're scared, but my mother taught me that it's important to tell the truth, even when you're scared."

The boy took a big gulp, then looked up at her. Then he reached into the seaweed and pulled out a shiny gold trident. **Princess Cressida** gasped. The merking's missing trident!

"I found it," the boy said. "I didn't know what it was, but when I picked it up and waved it around, the water started going crazy. Then everyone shouted that someone had stolen it, and I got scared, so I hid it."

"Don't be scared," said **Princess Cressida**. "If you tell the truth about what happened, it will be all right."

The merboy gave **Princess Cressida** the trident, and she swam quickly toward where the merking was floating next to his castle, watching the search with a worried frown.

"Your Majesty!" **Princess Cressida** shouted. "Your trident is here!"

"You found it!" **Princess Crystal** shouted joyfully, swimming up next to her father.

"No," said **Princess Cressida**, pointing toward the merboy. "He found it, but he was scared to tell anyone, in case they thought he stole it. He didn't mean any harm."

"I'm so happy to have it back," said the king, with a huge smile. He smiled at the merboy too. "You're not in trouble. I'm so glad you told the truth."

The king looked at **Princess Cressida** again. "Thank you for your help, **Princess Cressida**." He put an arm around his daughter's shoulders.

"I'm so glad that my daughter is your friend. I hope there will always be peace and friendship between our two kingdoms of the land and sea."

"Me too," said **Princess Cressida**, a happy smile on her face.

"And I think I'd better go home, before my parents wonder where I am."

"I'll swim with you," said **Princess Crystal**, linking arms with her friend.

The two princesses swam to the surface again.

"I'm sad to get out of the water," said **Princess Cressida**. "It's so beautiful in your underwater kingdom."

"Don't worry!" said **Princess Crystal**. "Now that you can turn into a mermaid, you can come back anytime you want! I'll show you all the amazing wonders of the ocean."

Princess Cressida hugged her friend. "I can't wait."

Then she turned and swam toward shore, back to her castle, her parents, and her home.

13

THE END